The Energy Bus for Kids

Published by John Wiley & Sons, Inc., Hoboken, New Jersey.
Published simultaneously in Canada.

For general information on our other products and services or for technical support, please contact our Customer Care Department within the United States at (800) 762-2974, outside the United States at (317) 572-3993 or fax (317) 572-4002.

Wiley publishes in a variety of print and electronic formats and by print-on-demand. Some material included with standard print versions of this book may not be included in e-books or in print-on-demand. If this book refers to media such as a CD or DVD that is not included in the version you purchased, you may download this material at http://booksupport.wiley.com. For more information about Wiley products, visit www.wiley.com.

ISBN 978-1-118-28735-4 (cloth); ISBN 978-1-118-33072-2 (ebk); ISBN 978-1-118-33472-0 (ebk);
ISBN 978-1-118-45822-8 (ebk); ISBN 978-1-118-33357-0 (ebk)

Printed in the United States of America.

10 9 8 7 6 5 4 3

THE ENERGY BUS FOR KIDS

A Story about Staying Positive and Overcoming Challenges

Jon Gordon

Illustrated by Korey Scott

WILEY

John Wiley & Sons, Inc.

It was Monday and Mondays were never good for George. He woke up tired and grumpy, as usual.

He had watched too much television last night.

He got hooked on a video game.

He went to bed too late and had another fight with his sister, Georgette.

His mom was upset because he was late for the bus and still hadn't eaten his breakfast.

"It's the most important meal of the day," she said.

George knew she was right but he was too tired and had to hurry to catch the bus.

As George ran to the bus stop with his heavy backpack, he could see bus #11 pulling away.

George was so upset he wanted to cry … but he didn't. He just put his head down and wondered what else could go wrong today.

6

Luckily, as the bus driver drove away she saw George, stopped the bus, and yelled out the window,

"I wouldn't leave you. Come on. Get on the bus."

This bus driver wasn't his usual bus driver. George had never seen her before. She said her name was Joy and she had the biggest smile he had ever seen. He told her his name was George and sat down in the first seat.

"What's got you down and what's with the frown?" Joy asked.

"Everything is going wrong," George said.

"That's okay, George. You're on my bus now. I call it the Energy Bus. Sit down and I'm going to teach you some rules that will take you on a positive ride through life."

"Are you ready to learn the first rule?" Joy asked. "If you are say yes three times."

George and all the kids on the bus then shouted,

9

Joy told the kids on the bus the first rule.

Rule #1: Create a Positive Vision.

"When you are on the bus going to school, think about having a great day. When you are on the bus going home, picture yourself having a great night. When you think about your future, imagine yourself accomplishing your goals and dreams," said Joy.

"If you can see it, you can create it. If you have a vision, then you also have the power to make it happen."

As George waited for class to begin, he thought about what Joy had said about *creating a positive vision*.

He imagined himself getting an A+ on his spelling test today and hitting a home run in his baseball game on Saturday. Then he remembered his teacher telling him the importance of writing down your goals and drawing pictures of them.

So, George took out a piece of paper and drew a picture of his spelling test with a big A+ at the top.

He also drew a picture of himself hitting a home run.

George knew the pictures would help him remember his positive visions, so he folded his drawings and put them in his pocket.

That afternoon as George walked on the bus, Joy gave him a big smile and asked him to sit in the first seat again so they could talk.

"How was school?" she asked. "Did you have a better day?"

"It was a little better," answered George. "I felt happier and I'm pretty sure I got at least an A on my spelling test, but after that I had to deal with a bunch of challenges."

"I tripped in the hallway while walking to class."

"I couldn't find my math workbook."

"A few of the mean kids were doing their usual mean things."

"I got hit in the face with a soccer ball and had to go to the nurse."

"It just wasn't a good day," said George.

15

"I understand," said Joy. "We all will face challenges in life. That's why it's so important to learn the next rule."

"If you want to know what it is say *yes* three times with me."

George and everyone on the bus shouted, "Yes!" "Yes!" "Yes!"

Rule #2: Fuel Your Ride with Positive Energy.

"What's positive energy?" asked George.

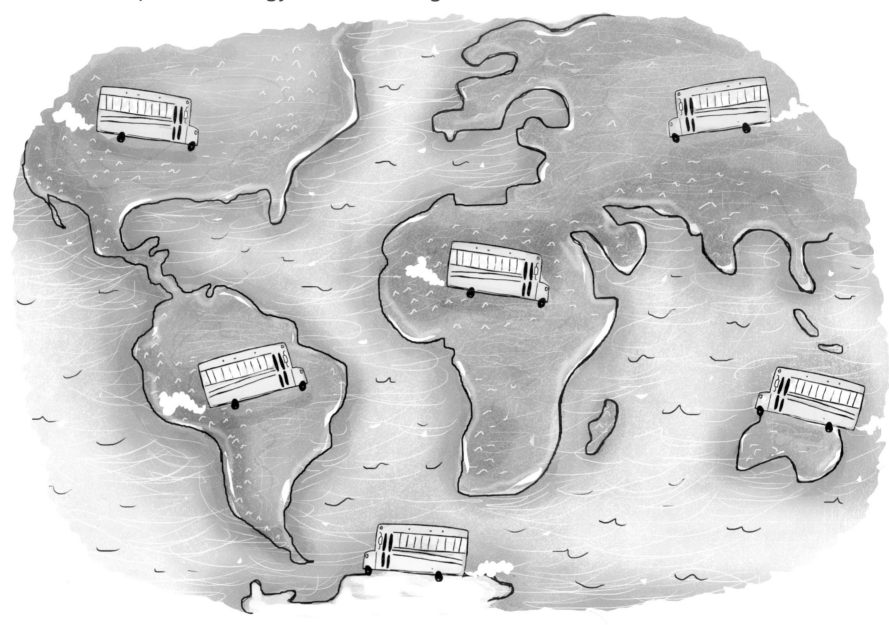

"It's the positive thoughts and emotions you think and feel and share with others," said Joy. "It is smiles, laughter, gratitude, trust, faith, joy, happy thoughts, and beliefs. If you fuel up with positive energy, you will have the power to overcome challenges and achieve your goals."

"But what if I *feel* negative?" asked George.

"Well that's the thing, George. You possess the greatest power in the world," said Joy.

"It's the power to choose to be positive instead of negative."

19

"So, what do you say we fuel up with lots of positive energy on our way home today?" asked Joy.

"Yes, Yes, Yes!" George and all the other students shouted.

The children cheered so loud the bus shook.

Then, as the Energy Bus approached George's bus stop, Joy told George to think of a success from his day and share it with his parents at dinner or bedtime. She said his success of the day could be one thing that made him smile and feel great.

The next morning George stepped onto the bus feeling more positive than ever.
"Someone is looking very happy today," Joy said, smiling at George.

"I feel like my tank is full of positive energy!"
George said with a big smile on his face.

"I love it, George! Make sure you keep filling your tank with positive energy throughout the day at school."
She gave him a few tips
to remember.

"Smile big.
Be thankful! And fuel
yourself with positive
beliefs."
Then she asked George to
repeat after her:
I am ready for a great day.
I believe in myself.
I trust that I will accomplish my goals and dreams.

The Energy Bus pulled up to the school and George stepped off, ready to take on the day. As he walked towards the building he heard Joy cheer.

"Remember, George, if you fuel up with positive energy you can go as far as you can dream ... Dream big, George!"

You would think that George stepped onto the bus that afternoon full of positive energy, but he didn't. Instead he walked on looking very sad and upset.

"What's the matter? What happened to my positive-energy guy?" Joy asked.

"I did everything you said. I fueled up with positive energy but that didn't stop the bullies at school from teasing me and embarrassing me," George said with tears in his eyes.

"I'm sorry you had to deal with bullies," said Joy. "I was bullied when I was a kid, and it didn't feel good."

Joy then raised her voice for the entire bus to hear and said, "Listen up, kids. DON'T BE A BULLY. Don't be mean. Don't say hurtful things to others. It will take you down the negative road of life. Instead, choose to be kind and travel down the positive road."

Joy then turned to George and said, "Bullies are just one of the many types of negative people you will face in life. Some may say negative things about you. Others feel so bad about themselves they try to make you feel bad, too. Rather than driving their own bus, they are trying to ruin everyone else's ride."

"That's why I always want you to remember the next rule," said Joy as she picked up a piece of paper from the dashboard and held it up for George and everyone to see.

Rule #3: No Bullies Allowed.

"This means you stay strong and positive and know that bullies can't drain your positive energy if you don't let their negativity into your mind. Negativity comes in many forms, but positivity is much more powerful than negativity. The key is to become more positive than the negativity you face."

"I understand," George said as the Energy Bus approached his bus stop. He walked off the bus realizing that he needed to be more positive than the bullies were negative. He also knew he needed a plan to neutralize the bullies and hoped Joy would have some ideas for him tomorrow.

The next morning when George got on the bus, he took his seat near Joy.
Joy smiled at him and told him that she had been thinking all night about how to deal
with bullies at school.

"Good, because I need a plan," said George.

"Well, I have a plan for you," said Joy.

"First, you avoid them. Do your best to stay away from any bullies that try
to zap your positive energy."

"Second, when they are mean to you, confront them and say, 'You are bullying me. Stop bullying me,' and walk away. Then, picture yourself driving your bus and shutting the door on them so they can't get on and their words can't affect your ride."

"Third, tell your parents, teacher, and principal. No one should have to deal with bullying. It's wrong."

"Okay, I'll try my best," said George as he walked off the bus towards the building where the bullies waited for him in the hallway.

When the bullies saw George, they began teasing him, but George was ready. He stayed positive, told himself to be strong, and told them to stop bullying him.

Then George pictured himself shutting the bus door on them and keeping them off his bus as he walked away. He could hear the teasing continue but he didn't let it bother him. In the past he had allowed them on his bus, but not today. Today he kept them off his bus and felt more positive than ever.

The minute the school bell rang, he ran to the bus to tell Joy. "It worked! It worked!" he cheered.

"I'm so happy for you," said Joy. "Positive energy is a powerful thing. And do you know what the most powerful form of positive energy in the world is?" asked Joy.

"I don't know," said George. "What?"

"It's LOVE and it's so powerful that it's part of the next rule I want to share with you."

Rule #4: Love Your Passengers.

"This means you become a powerful force of positive energy and share love with your passengers."

"Who are my passengers?" asked George.

"They are your fellow students, friends, teachers, siblings, family, and the people you interact with every day. Love everybody, George. Be kind. Help others. Make a difference."

"When you show kindness to others you attract kindness like a magnet. You surround yourself with so much positive energy that negativity doesn't even affect you," Joy said.

"Most importantly, when you put love into action, you change the world one loving act at a time."

The Energy Bus then pulled up to George's stop and as he walked away from the bus he waved to Joy and decided he was going to start showing kindness and love to his passengers at home.

That night, George spent extra time petting his dog.

He was kinder to his sister and told his mom he loved the dinner she made.

The next morning he made sure to wake up on time and eat his breakfast, knowing that would make his mom happy.

At school George smiled more and encouraged those who were having a bad day.

He shared his lunch with a girl who forgot her lunch at home.

He was extra kind to a girl that everyone teased and made her smile.

He helped a boy who dropped his books in the hallway.

George was so kind and positive that the bullies stayed away from him and he was surrounded by other positive kids.

When George walked on the bus that afternoon with a big smile on his face, he told Joy that he knew the next rule of the Energy Bus. "What's that, George?" she asked.

"It's to **enjoy the ride**," he said. He had learned that when you follow the Energy Bus rules you will enjoy the ride a whole lot more.

Rule #5: Enjoy the Ride.

George then pulled out a picture he had made in art class and gave it to Joy. She looked at the picture and smiled.

It was a picture that listed the five rules of the Energy Bus.

"I made one picture for you and one for our school," said George. "I shared the picture with our principal and now she's going to share the rules with all the teachers and students."

"Well, George, I will display this picture proudly on my bus for all my future passengers to see, and I will tell them about you and how you chose to fuel your life with positive energy."

Joy already knew what others would find out. George was no longer just a passenger on the bus.

He had become a positive driver who would change the world.

George would share the Energy Bus rules with others through his words and actions and they would learn what Joy taught him.

The Energy Bus will surely take you on the ride of your life.

Beep!   Beep!

The End.

A Message from George

When George was older he wrote some words to teach children the rules of the Energy Bus and inspire them to become drivers of their own bus. Here's what he wrote:

This is your Energy Bus!
You're the driver.
Did you know you can take your bus anywhere you want to go?
Say *yes* three times with me.
You can take it to college, your favorite place, or even the North Pole.
Just say where you want to go and believe that it will be so.

Every journey and ride begins with a positive vision to go somewhere and do something, and if you create a positive vision, then you also have the power to make it happen.

That's right. *You* have the power.

Your positive thoughts and beliefs are the fuel that powers your Energy Bus on your journey though life.

Your Energy Bus doesn't need gas.

"Yes!"

It runs on your positive energy, which includes your smiles, laughter, gratitude, faith, and positive beliefs and thoughts.

If you fuel up with positive energy your bus can go as far as you can dream. So are you ready for the ride of your life?

Smile big!
Think of a funny joke.
What are you thankful for?
Think of the one great thing
that happened today.
Dream about your future. What do you see?
If you see it, you can achieve it.

Ok, your tank is full. You are ready to step on the gas pedal and start driving towards your goals and dreams.

As you are driving, make sure you also watch out for obstacles on your journey. Every great driver will be tested. You'll likely face some challenges like flat tires. That's okay. Stay positive. Believe that everything happens for a reason. Learn from your setbacks, turn challenges into opportunities, and keep driving towards your destination.

"Yes!"

"Yes!"

You'll also surely face adversity. Everyone does. Adversity gives you a choice. You can give up on your journey, you can go down the negative road that leads to failure, or you can take the positive road to your goals and dreams. Choose the positive road.

Along the way you'll also face negative people called Bullies who can ruin your ride. Some of these people make fun of your dreams. Some may try to bully you with negative words. Others feel so bad about themselves they try to make you feel bad, too.

Negativity comes in all forms, but know this ... it is no match for your positivity.

Positivity is much more powerful than negativity.

So when you have someone try to get on your bus with their negativity, post a sign that says "No Bullies Allowed."

Don't let negative people ruin your ride.

Keep fueling up with positive energy.

If your positive energy, belief, and faith are greater than all the negativity you face, then nothing can stop you from reaching your destination.

Don't allow others to pressure you into letting them drive your bus. Be your own driver.

Stay positive and change the world.

I know you can do it. I believe in you.

COMPLIMENTARY RESOURCES

Visit

www.EnergyBusKids.com

for a free Discussion Guide and Activity Guide
for teachers and parents.

Utilize in the classroom or at home to reinforce the
principles and lessons found in this book.

Bring the Energy Bus to your School

Jon Gordon is passionate about developing positive schools, educators, and kids. He and his team of positive teachers have worked with countless school districts that have utilized The Energy Bus principles to enhance morale, improve teacher performance, and inspire students.

Programs include:

- Energy Bus Retreats for Principals
- Energy Bus Workshops for Teachers
- Readings in the Classroom with Illustrator Korey Scott
- Student Assemblies

For more information contact The Jon Gordon Companies at:

Phone: (904) 285-6842

Email: info@jongordon.com

Website: www.EnergyBusKids.com

 Facebook.com/JonGordonPage

@JonGordon11